Displaced Kingdom

A Minecraft Adventure

by S.D. Stuart

Summary

Episode 6:

The zombie Larissa is in pursuit of Suzy, leaving Josh to be captured by the mayor of Estermead. Separated from the others, Andre makes a startling discovery.

About S.D. Stuart's Minecraft Adventures:

With the wild success of the original novel, Herobrine Rises, (and the unrelenting demands from readers to know what happened next) S.D. Stuart's Minecraft Adventures has expanded into an ongoing series; with each new book written as an episode of a larger story.

Can ten-year-olds Josh, Andre, and Suzy stop the evil Herobrine from taking over the Minecraft world? Or will the real world be at the mercy of one of the most powerful video game bosses ever created?

Ramblin' Prose Publishing

Copyright © 2014 Steve DeWinter

www.SteveDW.com

Minecraft ® / TM & © 2009-2013 Mojang /
Notch

eBook Edition
ISBN-10:1-61978-022-4
ISBN-13:978-1-61978-022-4

Paperback Edition
ISBN-10:1-61978-023-2
ISBN-13:978-1-61978-023-1

Chapter 1

Larissa urged her dragon to fly faster, but Suzy was still moving away at a speed they just couldn't match. She heard a scream behind her and glanced back.

A baby dragon had a wriggling Andre in its talons and was struggling to remain airborne under the weight of its first capture. Andre looked down, realized he was hundreds of feet in the air, and instead of continuing to struggle, gripped the legs of the dragon and closed his eyes.

She scanned the skies ahead. Suzy was gone. There was no way she could catch up to her. Better to save Andre rather than risk losing both of them.

Larissa leaned back and they swopped down, twisting through the air until they were flying just under the baby dragon.

She called up to Andre. "Keep struggling.

When it lets go, I will catch you."

Andre looked down at her, then past her to the ground far below. "No way."

She held her hand out. "I will catch you."

Andre shook his head and gripped the dragon's leg tighter.

She sighed. If he wasn't going to let go on his own, she would have to force the baby dragon to drop him.

She shifted her weight, the dragon following her non-verbal instructions perfectly, and they rotated around through the air and settled into the space above the baby dragon.

Larissa's dragon screeched and dove straight for the other dragon. The baby dragon panicked and dropped Andre immediately.

Andre fell from the talons, screaming as he dropped like a rock toward the ground.

Larissa's dragon shot past the baby dragon. He pulled in his wings, trying to catch up with Andre. Larissa clung to his back, the wind threatening to knock her off.

Despite the wind trying to tear her off the dragon's back, she urged it to go faster. The ground was coming up fast, and it didn't look like they were going to reach Andre in time.

Chapter 2

Andre took another deep breath and used his full lungs to scream some more.

What was Larissa thinking? She had forced the dragon to let him go after she was no longer in position to catch him. Instead of dropping safely onto the back of her dragon, he was screaming toward the ground at terminal velocity.

He was spinning out of control and his view rotated from the fast approaching ground to Larissa struggling to catch up to him.

He twisted through the air, screaming. Larissa was still too far away to do anything to save him.

The first time he had fallen a great distance, he barely survived. Now he was falling five times farther than when he had jumped off that mountain. He wasn't going to make it this time.

When he hit the ground, he would use up all his health.

Notch had been wrong about so many things about this world.

What if when he died here, his heart just stopped beating in the real world? What if his brain reacted to the impact and he actually died?

Without him, they couldn't activate the crystal cube that would get them all safely out of this artificial world.

He stopped screaming and couldn't help laughing out loud as he plummeted to the ground.

Artificial!

Hah!

Everything about this world felt just as real as the world he had been born into. There was nothing artificial about it. Not the people, not the pain, and not death.

Was this it for him?

His mind played back snippets of his life.

Oh great, he thought, as his life flashed before his eyes.

His memory settled on a YouTube video he had seen with cartoon characters in a music video showcasing dumb ways to die.

Of all the dumb ways to die, this had to be the dumbest.

Chapter 3

Larissa clung tightly to her dragon. His wings were folded flat against his body and his feet were tucked in to reduce his profile. But it wasn't doing any good. They wouldn't be able to catch up with Andre before he hit the ground. They were getting too close to the ground themselves that if they didn't pull up soon, they would crash into the surface of the world along with him.

Larissa made the hardest decision of her life before it was too late for them too.

The dragon spread its wings and slowed quickly, arcing out across the tops of the trees as Andre disappeared into the forest at high speed.

Larissa circled around the forest, preparing herself for what she would see when she found Andre's body. Her hands were shaking as she guided her dragon toward the location she had seen him disappear.

She turned her head away as the dragon

landed.

Finally, she gathered enough courage to look at what was left of her friend.

She turned her head and her mouth gaped open in surprise.

Andre wasn't anywhere to be seen.

Instead of a crater where he would have impacted with the ground, the trees along one side of the clearing had been torn up at the roots and knocked aside. As she looked farther into the forest, there was a definite trail of destruction, like some giant had barreled through the forest, shoving aside everything in its path.

Did this have anything to do with Andre's disappearance?

It was too much of a coincidence not to.

If this had something to do with him, where was he?

Chapter 4

Nearly a minute before Larissa stared in disbelief at the odd destruction of the forest around her, Andre had closed his eyes as he passed the tops of the trees. He had mere milliseconds left to live before he hit the ground at full speed.

In that briefest of moments, his mind turned to who he would miss the most if this was truly the end. As Josh's face formed in his mind's eye, he smiled and suddenly rocketed sideways two feet above the ground.

He slammed into the trees, easily knocking them out of his way like they were made out of Styrofoam as he flew through the forest under his own power.

He rose up and shot out the tops of the trees, shooting over the forest.

He had figured out how to fly. But it wasn't because he had been trying to fly, it was pure instinct of survival. He didn't want to leave Josh alone and his mind had taken over, giving him powers he didn't think he would ever figure out.

He saw a hazy white streak across the sky, like the faint contrail left when a plane passes overhead. He didn't know why, but he knew that it was Suzy who had left these as she flew across the sky.

He hovered in the air. Should he go back and see if Josh was okay? Or should he go after Suzy?

Without having to think too hard about it, he shot off to follow the vapor trail.

Josh would be fine for a little while on his own.

Chapter 5

Tied to a bed, Josh bit down hard on the leather strap in his mouth as the redstone electricity coursed through his body.

Mayor Basia waved her hand. A guard flipped the lever and the electrical current shut off.

Josh's muscles relaxed and he sunk into the bed, sweating profusely while a single tear rolled down his cheek.

Basia stood over him. "What does Herobrine want with all the dragons?"

Josh shook his head and mumbled through the strap in his mouth. "I don't know."

She looked over at the guard and took a step back.

Josh twisted his head to plead with the guard. He couldn't see the guards face through the mask of his helmet. "Please don't."

The guard looked away from him and flipped the lever.

Josh's back arched as the electricity contracted every muscle in his body. She nodded at the guard and the electricity stopped burning through him. He relaxed against the restraints again.

She leaned over him. "I'll give you one more chance to..."

She was cut off by an explosion in the distance followed by more explosions and shouting. Another guard rushed through the door, removed his helmet, and bowed quickly to one knee in front of her.

"Mayor Basia."

"What is it, Commander?"

He stood up and snapped to attention. "Creepers are attacking the city ma'am."

She shot a look at Josh. "They're coming to rescue you."

She motioned to the guard standing near the lever. "Protect him with your life."

The guard bowed low and she rushed out of

the room with the commander following behind her.

Once the guard was alone with Josh, he ran forward and pulled at the straps that bound Josh's hands and feet to the bed. As soon as he was free, the guard helped Josh sit up.

Josh looked at him. "What are you doing?"

The guard glanced at the door to the room. "We need to get out of here before they discover that the Creepers on the other side of the city were nothing but a diversion."

"A diversion? For what?"

"To get you out of here."

"Who are you?"

The guard removed his helmet. Josh did a double-take as he looked into the eyes of Herobrine. They didn't glow in this world like they did in the game, but there was no mistaking who he was looking at.

And who was saving him.

"Why are you helping me?"

"I have a problem. It seems that the Creeper army has chosen you as their leader and they won't do anything I tell them. I got them to agree to the distraction only because I promised to rescue you and bring you back."

Josh frowned as Herobrine helped him stand. He was unsteady on his feet from being electrocuted.

"If you are here to save me, why did you dress up like a guard and help the mayor do all this to me?"

Herobrine shrugged his shoulders. "I had to wait for the attack. I must say, I'm impressed with how long you held out. You didn't give her any information no matter how much she tortured you."

Josh stumbled as they walked toward the door and held onto Herobrine for support. "That's because I don't know anything."

Herobrine smiled. "Interesting. Notch didn't tell you why you are here?"

Josh leaned heavily on Herobrine. "He sent us in to get you."

Herobrine nodded. "Very interesting. I have something to show you."

"What is it?"

"All in due time my boy. But first, I need you to tell my army to follow my orders."

Chapter 6

Andre followed the dissipating trail until he couldn't see it any more ahead of him. He hovered in the air looking in every direction for some indication of which way Suzy had gone.

At this height, he was well above the clouds and couldn't see the ground. Why was she flying so high above the world?

He looked back the way he had come. The trail was barely visible. If he wasn't looking straight along it, he wouldn't have been able to see it. As he watched, the last of the stark white ribbon of water vapor faded away. It was only when the trail disappeared completely did he realize he had been so focused on following it, he hadn't been paying attention to where he was going and now had no idea where he was.

He hovered in circles, disoriented. Only when he realized he had been chasing Suzy toward the setting sun did he regain his bearings. He shot off in the direction he figured Suzy was headed. If she had dropped below the clouds, he would never find her. But there had to be a reason she had been traveling so high up.

Chapter 7

Suzy hid silently among the clouds, watching Andre head off in the direction she had gone before slowing down enough to not leave behind a contrail.

So, he had finally learned how to fly. It didn't matter. Herobrine had given her explicit instructions should she be unable to get the dragons from Basia.

She waited until Andre disappeared in the distance before leaving the thick cloud. She headed off at a right angle to the direction Andre had flown. By the time he decided she had not gone that way, she would be somewhere else. He would not find her again until she was ready to be found. And by then, it would be too late to stop what Herobrine had planned.

Chapter 8

Andre flew quickly, lost in thought, and nearly crashed into the side of a mountain. Surprisingly, the tip of the mountain was above him. He hadn't even realized he had been flying upside down as he shifted his perspective and headed for the bottom of the mountain.

He followed the mountain to its base only to discover it terminated high in the sky and wasn't connected to the ground far below. As he passed the edge, he was shocked to discover a city built along the underside. How had someone built a city under a mountain?

He noticed the setting sun, and realized he hadn't been upside down. The mountain was. When he righted himself, he realized he was looking at a city floating high in the clouds. The section of ground it had been built on tapered down to a point after being ripped from the surface and raised a mile into the sky; separated from the world below.

He hovered along the edge of the city. Of the buildings he could see on this side, they all looked very old with most of them crumbling to rubble in disrepair. Slowly, he floated into the city, hovering a hundred feet above the streets below. As he traveled between the collapsing buildings, there were no signs of life anywhere. Whatever had become of the occupants of this city had happened a long time ago.

A piece of building dislodged itself and crashed down to the surface of the floating island. He circled around and thought he saw a shadow move in his peripheral vision. He glanced in the direction of the shadow and thought he heard something, but there was nothing there but shadows and decay.

Another piece of building crumbled behind him.

He spun around, still floating in the air, and saw a huge net flying through the air toward him.

Before he could react, the net engulfed him and zapped him with electricity. His stomach lurched as he fell.

He plummeted to the ground inside the netting, unable to do anything but brace for impact.

Chapter 9

Suzy flew back to the cave entrance, angry with herself for not being able to bring back a dragon egg. There were two ways to control a dragon. The first was to possess a rare crystal that made the dragon follow your orders. The other was to be the first person it sees when it hatches.

Since the dragons had hatched together unexpectedly, it stood to reason that they had only seen each other. Now, the only way to control a dragon was to find the source of the crystals. And only Herobrine knew where that was.

A thought occurred to her.

If she could figure out which dragon was the first to hatch, she could control it with a crystal; and all the other dragons would follow. She would be able to command an entire army of dragons simply by controlling the first dragon.

As soon as she was back, she would ask Herobrine how to determine which dragon was the first.

She landed softly next to the cave entrance. She was getting the hang of flying. It was going to be hard to go back to only being able to walk and run when she returned to the real world. Flying was so liberating. And it was definitely the only way to get around.

The iron golems watched her as she passed between them, but since Herobrine had already told them that she was with him, they didn't make a move to stop her.

She walked into the cave and headed for the lower levels where Herobrine would be waiting for her to return.

As she got closer, she could hear Herobrine discussing the Creeper army with someone else. The other person's voice was instantly familiar. Could it be?

She walked around the corner and saw Josh

and Herobrine staring down at Josh's open map, debating with each other while pointing at various locations on the map.

She couldn't keep from gasping out in surprise at seeing Josh.

They looked up from the map and Josh smiled. "Suzy!"

He jumped up and ran to her, hugging her tightly.

She hugged him back, actually happy to see him.

She held him back at arm's length. "What are you doing here?"

Josh motioned to Herobrine with his head. "I'm joining with you and Herobrine."

"What?"

"I want to help, just like you."

"You don't know..."

He cut her off. "Suzy, all of humanity is going to be enslaved. And if joining with Herobrine is the only way to keep everyone I care about safe;

then I'm in."

She looked over at Herobrine. "You showed him?"

Herobrine nodded.

"How much?"

"Everything."

She looked back at Josh. "This isn't going to be easy."

Josh smiled. "Nothing worth doing ever is."

Chapter 10

Andre woke with a start when someone poked him in the ribs with a stick. He was still tangled in the net lying on the ground. He heard the voices of several people standing around him. He stayed perfectly still, listening to them.

"The auto trap must be malfunctioning. This isn't a dragon," someone said.

"Look at his clothes. He's not from around here."

"So?"

"So, if he didn't come on a dragon, how did he get up here from the surface, let alone be high enough to trigger the trap?"

The crowd fell quiet for a minute until a new voice broke the silence.

"The Oracle will know how he got here. She might even know who he is."

Several voices grunted in agreement until someone spoke up.

"What if she doesn't?"

He was immediately reprimanded.

"Don't let her hear you speak like that! She knows everything."

"Do you think it's safe to take him to her first? What if he is with the enemy?"

"You're right. We should take him to see Paul first. He will get the intruder to talk."

Andre had heard enough. He wasn't going to let them take him anywhere. Everyone jumped back when he sat up under the net. He pulled the netting off of him as he stood up.

Everyone backed away leaving an empty circle of space around Andre.

He spun around slowly, looking at everyone in turn. "Who's in charge?"

A brave onlooker spoke up. "Mallory is our leader."

He looked around at the faces in the crowd. "Which one of you is Mallory?"

The same brave speaker stepped forward. "He

is not here. We speak to him through the Oracle."

Andre frowned at that statement. "Is there someone I can actually see who runs things around here?"

The speaker for the group took another step forward. "I can take you. Who should I tell him is asking to speak with him?"

Finally, they were getting somewhere. "Tell him Andre wants to speak with him."

The speaker turned around. "Follow me."

Andre followed the speaker. The rest of the crowd followed, not letting him out of their sight.

The group walked into a building that was half fallen over, the top half leaning against the building next to it. The whole city looked like a big post-apocalyptic movie set.

As they walked through the dark building, everyone they came across stopped whatever they were doing to gawk at the stranger.

Andre felt nervous with how everyone seemed shocked to silence when he walked past them.

"Why is everyone staring at me?" he asked the group around him in general.

The speaker turned his head to look at Andre. "We don't get people visiting our city too often. Come to think of it, we never get visitors that aren't trying to attack and take over the city."

Andre looked at the decay and filth all around him. "Why would anyone want this place?"

"Our city is special. We can communicate with a world that is outside our own."

Andre stopped suddenly, everyone else stopping with him. "This city is an access point?"

The speaker's eyebrows knitted in confusion. "Access point? What is that?"

Andre looked around at the faces that surrounded him in the semi-darkness of the hallway. "What do you mean that you can communicate outside this world?"

The speaker was about to say something when

the look on his face shifted to one of fear. "Daniel can explain it better than I."

"Then take me to Daniel."

"This way." The speaker turned and walked down the hallway. Andre followed him to a small door where he stood waiting. As soon as Andre was closer, the speaker opened the door and motioned for Andre to go through.

Andre stepped into an empty room and the speaker closed the door behind him. Andre heard the locks engage. He thought about breaking the door down with his newfound strength, but he wanted to see what these people knew about the access point. He looked around the small room. The wallpaper had peeled away and the walls behind it had developed cracks and holes.

"Who are you?"

The voice behind him startled him. He spun around and looked at a floating distorted video image of a high school aged kid's face wearing headphones looking back at him.

"Who are you?" the voice demanded again, the hint of a Russian accent evident in the kid's speech.

Andre gulped and stood to his full height. "My name is Andre. Who are you?"

"I'm David, ruler over Sky City. Where did you come from?"

Andre thought about telling him about Notch, the brainwave helmets, and Herobrine. Instead, he decided to play it like he was a local game entity.

"Estermead."

David looked down and Andre could hear him typing furiously. He looked back up. "I don't see a dragon nearby. How did you get up to the city?"

"I flew."

The kid laughed. "You can't fly."

"I can."

"How? There is no mod running on this

server."

Andre decided it was time to tell this kid a part of the truth.

"I'm not from here, originally."

"Okay, I'll bite. Where are you from, originally?"

"I'm just like you."

"You are not like me."

"True. You have to use a webcam to be seen in this world, while I can inhabit an avatar."

David looked at him closely. "How do you know about webcams?"

"Because I am from the real world, like you."

David stared at him and then the floating image of his face winked out of existence.

Andre looked around the room. "David?"

He waited a few moments.

He did not respond.

"David?"

Nothing.

He walked over to the door and twisted the

knob.

Locked.

He pulled on the door, ripping it from the hinges. He set the door to the side and stepped back out into the hallway.

The speaker was there, pointing a strange looking device at him. "Don't move."

Andre laughed. "Or you'll what?"

The speaker pulled on the trigger and tendrils of lightning shot out the open end of the device and engulfed Andre.

Every muscle locked up and Andre fell to the floor, stiff as a board.

David's image appeared over him. "I checked. There is no one else logged in to this server. Not only is the server unlisted, it took every one of my hacking skills just to get in, so no one but me could be logged in. I ask again. Who are you?"

Andre spoke through gritted teeth, his jaw refusing to move. "I told you, I am human, just like you."

The image swooped up to face the speaker. "Take him to the communication room. And increase security. He might be an indicator that an attack is coming."

The speaker yanked Andre off the ground and tossed him over his shoulder. "Yes sir."

The image floated behind Andre as he was carried out of the building.

David smiled at him. "Paul will find out who programmed you. Or you will die while he attempts to get the truth out of you."

Chapter 11

Herobrine watched as Josh checked over the Creeper army. A sudden loud tone filled the entire cavern, echoing off the walls and ceiling. Herobrine looked at Josh. "I will be right back."

Herobrine walked into a large room with a single chair at the center, surrounded by redstone equipment. He sat in the chair quickly and closed his eyes.

He was instantly transported to the empty white space where he communicated with those outside.

"What is it Walter?"

Walter's voice echoed all around him. "I have traced an intruder to your world."

"Where is he?"

"He is at the nearest access point."

"The floating city?"

"Yes. How many dragons have hatched?"

"The signal you transmitted resulted in all of

them hatching, but I have been unable to get them yet. Josh is preparing the Creeper army for an assault on Estermead to free the dragons for our main attack on the floating city. We will have the dragons by sunrise tomorrow."

"Good. I will have dragon riders programmed and loaded into the world by then. What is your plan?"

"Each dragon will carry four Creepers up to the floating city. Once the Creepers have begun taking out the defenses, we can send in the main invasion force, capture any survivors, and move them off the island. We will control the access point within an hour of launching the first Creeper attack."

"Excellent. Notch had no idea how useful you would become when he created you from a military strategy program. What of the humans sent in to stop you?"

"Two of them are working for me now."

"Good. And the third?"

"I do not know where he is."

"Could he be a problem?"

"Even if he could stop me on his own, which I doubt, he has no idea which access point I will strike first. And even if he did, he could never get up there to do anything about it."

"You seem confident in your success."

"The girl, Suzy, assures me that she was the only one to learn how to fly and Josh confirmed this. The other boy will not be a problem."

"Then you have my permission to proceed at the earliest possible moment. Eve is about to come online, and we need to be ready."

Herobrine bowed his head. "I understand."

The stark white scene faded around him, leaving him sitting in the chair in the midst of the redstone equipment.

It was time to prepare for the attack on Estermead.

Chapter 12

Andre was dropped roughly on the floor in an empty room. He was still frozen solid, and only when he heard the door close behind him and several locks engaged did he know that he had been left alone.

The room flashed brightly several times and he found he could move again.

He sat up and looked around at the room. There was nothing in it, and it was the first place that was sparkling clean. David's face appeared in front of him.

"Have a seat," David commanded.

Andre looked around at the empty room. "On what?"

David looked down and Andre could hear him typing furiously. A chair appeared in the middle of the room. David looked at him again. "Sit."

Andre crossed his arms. "Say please."

David's face grew red with anger. "Sit!"

Andre put a hand against his ear and cocked his head to the side, exaggerating the motions of listening. "I didn't hear a please."

David looked down again and typed loudly. The room flashed white and Andre collapsed to the floor under the weight of an unseen force.

David's face hovered over him. "I can increase the gravity more and flatten you like a pancake. Are you going to sit in the chair, or do I turn you into the main ingredient of an IHOP Pancake Platter breakfast?"

Andre grunted unintelligibly.

David's face moved in closer to the webcam, the distortion of the lens making his nose expand faster than his face. "What was that?"

Andre called out with considerable effort. "Yes."

"Yes what?"

"Yes... chair... sit."

The room flashed white and the pressure on

Andre's body instantly disappeared. He rolled over onto his stomach and coughed. He sat up on his knees and looked at the image of David floating in front of him.

David's eyes shifted in the direction of the chair.

Andre stood up and walked over, sitting down in the chair.

David smiled. It was not a warm smile.

"Now that we have established that I am more powerful than you, I need you to put on the helmet." He glanced down and typed.

A machine appeared in the corner, wires snaking to a helmet that appeared on a small table that was suddenly next to the chair. David looked at Andre.

"Put it on, please."

"Finally, some civility," Andre muttered as he reached for the helmet.

David laughed. "I just don't have the patience to force you again. I might end up killing you by accident. And then where would we be? This is faster."

Andre strapped the helmet to his head. "What are you going to do to me?"

David was focused on the keyboard out of sight of the webcam.

"I want to look at your program."

"I'm not a program."

David looked up and smiled. "Everyone but me is a program. Surprisingly, you are aware of the world outside, but don't know you are a program."

"Because I'm not."

"Let's see who programmed you to think you are a real boy."

David's face disappeared and Andre felt a tingling sensation start in his head and spread throughout his body. He reached up to remove the helmet, but his arms refused to respond as they stayed motionless at his side.

He felt his mind expand and contract in

pulses. He didn't know how else to describe the sensation of another person accessing his memories. He wasn't a computer program, and the human mind wasn't designed to be treated like one. What could this do to him?

The pulsing stopped and was replaced with nothing.

The room around him was gone.

He looked down.

Even his body was gone.

All he could see was never ending white space that either stretched out to infinity, or ended mere inches from his face.

A voice echoed inside his head. Or was it echoing inside the white space?

He couldn't tell.

"My name is Paul and I would like to ask you a few questions."

Chapter 13

Mayor Basia looked at the damage to her horse stables. To make matters worse, the first dragon to hatch had become strong enough to escape. It wouldn't be long before the rest could break through the bars of their cages.

It had been her experience that dragons were solitary creatures, and usually spent as much time away from other dragons as possible. However, these dragons were behaving differently. In fact, ever since the first dragon had gone missing, the rest of the dragons had become increasingly restless.

Nothing her men tried would calm them down. They were going to break out of their cages soon, and there was nothing she could do about it. She thought about letting them out before they tore her stables to shreds, but the thought of forty dragons terrorizing the countryside was not something she was prepared to deal with, let alone the impact on the local economy.

She saw no other choice.

She would have to destroy the dragons before it was too late.

She turned to the captain of her guard. "I need your men to burn down the stables."

The captain looked at her with a shocked expression on his face. "What about the dragons?"

"They are to be destroyed as well."

"But…"

She cut him off. "If they cannot be controlled, then they must be eliminated."

He bowed his head slightly. "Yes ma'am."

She stomped away, knowing that her orders would be followed to the letter.

Chapter 14

Fernando, the Captain of the Guard watched as Mayor Basia walked away. He couldn't believe that she had ordered the destruction of such magnificent creatures.

He looked at the destroyed frame of the door. If only one dragon could do this to solid oak and iron, what could forty of them do?

And what happened when they had babies, and there were hundreds, possibly even thousands, of dragons roaming the countryside?

The mayor was right. They had to do something now before it got out of hand.

He was about to find his second in command when an explosion drew his attention to the eastern wall. A plume of smoke rising above it.

They were being attacked again.

But who was attacking them this time?

Fernando ran toward the plume of smoke and heard more explosions come from different sections of the wall. Whoever was attacking was doing so in several places at once.

He recognized the type of explosions as he got closer to the inner wall and he could hear the unmistakable hiss that preceded each explosion.

Creepers were attacking the city.

But they were doing so in greater numbers than ever before. His ears were ringing from the incessant explosions all around the city, leaving everyone running around, and into each other, as panic grew among the citizens.

Fernando called out, trying to retain a semblance of order. "Everyone go to the shelters at the center of town!"

More explosions echoed around the city when he heard someone scream, "They broke through the outer wall!"

The people around him all started screaming, and nobody could hear anything he said anymore as they ran back and forth in a blind panic.

People were starting to get knocked down as

everyone rushed to be the first to the shelters.

Fernando called out, "Everyone remain calm!" But it was no use. No one listened to him.

He wasn't doing much good here. He had to get to the front lines and help repel the attacking Creepers. He spun in a slow circle and saw plumes of smoke rising in every direction. There were no front lines in this battle. The Creepers were attacking from every angle with Estermead as their focal point.

A multitude of crashing sounds drew his attention back to the stables. The dragons had broken free of their cages and were now curiously peeking out through the main doors.

This wasn't good.

Another explosion, closer this time, spooked the dragons and a few of them ran out into the crowded street.

If the people running around weren't already panicking before, as soon as they saw the horse-sized dragons lumbering toward them, they were certainly panicking now.

If it were possible, the crowd screamed even louder as they surged away from the dragons like ocean waves pulling away from the beach at low tide.

A dragon squawked loudly, with the other dragons returning its call. As they all squawked louder in response to each other, more dragons spilled out of the stables until they crowded the streets.

Fernando's head spun.

He didn't know what to do first. Which of the multiple situations forming around him was the most critical? The Creepers attacking? The throngs of people tripping over each other as they ran in every direction at once? Or the growing group of dragons that were all squawking loudly while snapping at each other as more came out of the stables?

He backed away from the dragons as they began walking down the street toward him. What

Mayor Basia had asked him to do was no longer an option. The dragons were no longer contained inside their cages in the stables.

And the city was defenseless against them. Not only could they fly, but they were already inside the walls.

His head was pounding from the constant noise of explosions, people screaming, and dragons calling to the sky, when it suddenly fell eerily silent.

The dragons all stopped screeching at the same time and stopped to listen to something. But what?

The explosions around the city had also stopped and Fernando was worried that he had become deaf since he couldn't hear anything but the steady beat of his heart.

And then he heard it.

A faint call by some bird high in the sky.

The dragons all reacted by calling back in the same tone.

Fernando craned his neck and saw a dragon circling the city. It responded again to the cries of those on the ground with one of its own.

This excited the dragons and, one by one, they took to the sky to join the dragon already circling overhead.

In less than a minute, the last of the dragons had left the stable and joined those already circling the city like some dark, evil, tornado.

When the last of the dragons were circling the city, one of the dragons broke from the swirling mass and flew away from the city. The rest of the dragons followed, and soon, the sky was clear again, except for the smoke from the fires.

But the Creepers had stopped as well.

Why had they stopped?

Fernando ran toward the closest guard tower and quickly climbed the stairs, taking two at a time.

He found the master guard at the top, who barked orders to other guards right before they took off down the stairs past Fernando.

He approached the master guard.

"Did any Creepers get into the city?"

The master guard shook his head. "They stopped right before getting in and left."

"That doesn't make any sense."

"You're telling me. There had to a thousand Creepers lining up against the wall. If they all went off at the same time, we would have lost the inner wall in a matter of seconds. Instead, they all turned and left."

"What about the outer wall?"

"The reports I'm getting are confusing. They did break through, but the damage was localized to specific areas that we can easily repair. It's like they knew where to hit us without causing too much damage."

"That is strange. Why would they care about that?"

"I try not to think like a Creeper if I can help it," the master guard replied.

"When, exactly, did the Creepers stop their advance into the city?"

"About the same time that dragon in the sky showed up."

Fernando nodded. "Why did they all leave at the same time?"

Chapter 15

Suzy tucked the glowing purple crystal back into the folds of her cloak as she hovered hundreds of feet in the air.

She had watched the swelling mass of dragons circle the city and then break off to all follow one dragon.

That had to be the first dragon.

But before she could control all the dragons, she had to control one of them. And that wasn't going to be easy.

She shot forward through the air on a course that would take her to the first dragon. She flew higher in the air, hoping that, like most birds of prey, the dragons would keep watch below them, but not worry too much about what was happening above them.

She wanted to extend the time she had before they spotted her. She had to retain the element of surprise for as long as possible. Hopefully she would be practically on top of her target before he noticed she was there. She was certain that he would not surrender willingly, or easily. And those following him would most likely strive to protect him.

She looked at the swirling dragons as they flew through the sky below. There sure were a lot of them. She steadied her nerves and dropped down, coming in at an oblique angle to avoid being detected before she landed on top of the lead dragon.

She held her arms tightly at her side as she rocketed straight for the dragon's back. Right before she made contact, the dragon shifted to the side and she flew right past it.

The two dragons flying beside him screeched loudly in protest of the sudden intruder and dove after her. She glanced back just as a dragon slashed at her with its hind claws.

She rolled to the side and dropped out of reach; temporarily. She didn't have wings, and relied on gravity to fall as fast as she could go.

She had been so focused on the one dragon, she nearly missed seeing the other dragon that was coming straight at her. At the last second, she rolled tightly into a ball as the dragon slammed into her, sending her spiraling off in another direction; unconscious.

Her body unspooled slowly as she fell. The two dragons chasing her slowed their descent. They tracked her with their eyes until she splashed into the lake below.

As she slowly sunk beneath the surface, they circled slowly, watching for any sign of her resurfacing.

When she didn't come back up, they flew toward the receding group of dragons, their job of protecting their leader complete.

Chapter 16

Larissa was returning to Estermead, after losing Andre, when she spotted the darkened cloud against the horizon that ebbed and flowed as it traveled along the peaks of the mountains.

Her dragon bucked under her, nervous about the moving shape in the distance. Larissa slowed her dragon and hovered in the air, trying to see what caused the dark cloud when two smaller shapes broke free.

She raised a green hand over her red eyes and squinted. She realized that she wasn't looking at a cloud, but a bunch of dragons all flying together. Those must be the dragons from Estermead.

Her eye noticed a tiny dot being pursued by two of the dragons. It looked like a person. But the only one she knew who could fly was Suzy.

Larissa nudged her dragon in the sides with her boots and flew straight for the battle taking place in the sky.

She was still too far away to help when Suzy slammed into the water and sank below the surface. By the time she reached the lake's edge, the other two dragons had rejoined the swirling dark cloud.

She flew low over the surface, following the ripples that had formed when Suzy hit the water to their center. She pulled her dragon into the air and then somersaulted into a dive.

She held on tight as the surface of the water tried to yank her from the back of her dragon as they dove into the water after Suzy.

Her dragon cupped his wings as he propelled himself through the water and up to a still sinking Suzy.

Larissa wrapped her arm around Suzy and held her tight as they rose up through the water.

The three of them broke the surface, water splashing all around them.

The dragon landed along the lake's edge.

Larissa jumped off and laid Suzy down softly on the sandy shore and stared intently at her.

Suzy laid on the sand perfectly still; not breathing or moving at all. If she was dead, there was only one thing Larissa could do to bring her back.

She licked her lips in anticipation. She had to resist taking too big of a bite. She wanted to keep Suzy alive by turning her into a zombie, not have her for lunch.

She leaned over Suzy, baring her teeth and lowering herself slowly, her mouth widening as she got closer.

Suzy's eyes popped open. "What are you doing?" she asked.

Larissa sat back. "You're alive!"

"What happened?"

"You were knocked out by a dragon and fell into the water. I thought you had drowned."

"So, you were going to zombify me?"

Larissa smiled, her sharp teeth glistening. "It

would have worked; I think."

Suzy sat up. "You think?"

"I'm new to this. You had only just died, so there was a small possibility I could bring you back. Wait? How are you still alive?"

Suzy looked around. "I don't know."

She turned to Larissa. "Take me back."

"Where are we going?"

"We're taking them back to Herobrine."

Larissa's face grew somber. "Why?"

"We need these to attack the access point."

"Why are you taking these to him? He's a monster."

"He's not a monster…"

Larissa interrupted her and held her arms wide. "Look what he did to me! He made me a monster!"

"I thought your mother bit you?"

"She did. But who do you think made her into a monster? He did."

"You don't have to come with me if you don't

want to."

Larissa shook her head. "No. I want to ask him why he did this. To her. To me. He is my father. I should give him the chance to explain himself."

Suzy smiled. "When he shows you what he has planned, you will understand why he did what he did. You might even be able to help him."

"I don't get it. When we first met, you were working to stop him. Now you are working for him? What changed?"

Suzy looked into the distance at nothing. "He showed me what would happen to my world and gave me a choice."

"So you chose to follow him?"

Suzy looked back at Larissa. "I chose to live."

Chapter 17

Andre sat slumped over in the chair. He was exhausted. He had been answering Paul's questions as truthfully as he could for over an hour.

And since Paul was a software program from outside the Minecraft world, it didn't hurt to tell him about Herobrine, their mission, or who they really were.

Paul had finally released him a few minutes ago, and the first thing Andre did was yank the helmet off his head.

David's image appeared in front of him.

"It looks like you were telling the truth. I'm surprised Notch made it so you could enter this world as an avatar."

Andre looked up at the floating image. "Why is that so surprising?"

David's face showed a hint of anger. "Because he wouldn't do it for me."

Andre's eyes widened in surprise. "You know Notch?"

"Yes. In fact, he sent me in here to protect the access points should Herobrine ever get into this world. You and I are on the same mission."

Andre massaged his aching muscles. "Then why did you torture me like that?"

"I had to be sure."

"You could have just asked."

"We didn't have that much time. So your friend Suzy is working for Herobrine now?"

Andre nodded. "Yeah. He must have brainwashed her or something."

"What about Josh?"

"I don't know. The baby dragon took me when he was still in the city. He either got away, or the mayor captured him, or worse, Herobrine captured him."

David nodded. "Then we have to assume that they are both working for Herobrine."

"What?! Why are you assuming that?"

"Herobrine can be very convincing when he wants to be."

"How do we save them?"

"First, we have to…" A beeping tone came from off screen and David moved out of view. He came back quickly.

"We'll talk later."

The floating image of him disappeared.

"Wait!" Andre yelled, but it was no use.

David was gone.

Andre stood up on shaky legs. He was feeling his strength returning. Soon, he would be able to fly again. And then he would get off this floating city and find his brother.

And find out why Suzy was helping the enemy.

He knew they should never have let her join them. She had been nothing but trouble ever since they had arrived. And now she was working against them.

Who knew what kind of trouble she was

getting herself into now that she didn't have him to stop her?

Chapter 18

Suzy clung to the underside of Larissa's dragon as they flew under the formation of dragons toward the front of the group.

Suzy's thought that the baby dragons would not attack an adult dragon was correct, and they were able to fly among the dragons without interference.

As they neared the front, Larissa pulled her dragon higher, bringing Suzy directly over the lead dragon.

It was now or never, Suzy thought, as she let go and dropped onto the back of the lead dragon.

The dragon reacted immediately by spinning upside down and wriggling, trying to knock off whatever had just landed on its back.

Suzy clung tightly and stroked the dragon's neck while making soothing sounds. The crystal around her neck glowed brightly and a thread of sparkling light wound through the air and into the back of the dragon's head.

The dragon quickly righted itself and stopped trying to buck Suzy off of it.

She was now in control of the lead dragon.

She held the ridges along the side of his neck like handle bars on a bicycle and directed which way she wanted to go by pulling them gently one way or another. He wheeled around in a circle, heading back in the direction of Herobrine's underground lair.

The entire group of dragons followed suit.

She was now in control of all the dragons.

Larissa pulled alongside her. "Feels great, doesn't it?"

Suzy nodded. "I never in a million years thought I would be riding my very own dragon."

Reaching their destination, Suzy landed her dragon in the clearing in front of the cave. She hopped off, patting him on the side of the neck. "Good boy."

Larissa, and the rest of the dragons, all landed in the clearing, quickly crowding the open space.

The two iron golems watched Suzy approach with Larissa by her side. Suzy hooked a thumb in her direction. "She's with Herobrine too."

They both walked into the cave entrance unhindered. Suzy glanced at Larissa. "They're not too bright, but at least they follow orders."

When they reached the main chamber of the cave, Josh came running over. "You're back."

He looked past Larissa and then back to her. "Where's Andre?"

She shook her head. "I lost him."

We need to find him quickly. He ran over to the table where the crystal cube sat. He held it up and it barely glowed in his hand. "We don't have much time left to help Herobrine and then get home. Did you get the dragons?"

Suzy nodded. "All of them. We can launch an attack on the access point at any time."

A voice echoed from across the chamber.

'Excellent."

Herobrine walked over to them. He glanced briefly at the cube that Josh was setting on the table. "Josh, prepare the Creeper army."

Josh nodded. "Yes sir."

He ran off and disappeared into a darkened tunnel.

Herobrine turned to Suzy. "Get the golems to help you bring food and water to the dragons. We need them ready to fly to the access point without stopping. Our best chance is a speedy attack."

Suzy ran off toward the entrance.

Herobrine faced Larissa. "When this is over, we will talk about your mother."

A tear formed along the edge of her eyes. "You killed her."

"I loved her."

Larissa held her green hands up. "You turned us into this."

Herobrine's face grew sad. "I did what needed

to be done."

"Hah! So you could continue your conquest of this world, and the world beyond?"

He let out a sigh. "Come with me."

"Why?"

"There's someone you need to meet."

"Who?"

He held out his hand. "He's the one who showed me who I really was. He's the one who told me what I needed to do."

She took his hand and let him lead her to a door at the edge of the underground chamber.

Chapter 19

Larissa followed Herobrine through the door into a room filled with redstone equipment connected to a chair in the middle of the room.

He motioned to the chair. "Have a seat, Larissa."

She sat down and the room started spinning. She jumped up from the chair and Herobrine grabbed her arm, tenderly guiding her back to the chair.

"The first time is a little disorienting. You'll be okay."

She sat back down again and the room swirled around her before fading to white.

She suddenly found herself in a stark white space.

A voice boomed from every direction at once.

"Who are you?"

She cleared her throat and replied nervously. "My name is Larissa."

"Ahh, Herobrine's daughter. I am sorry to hear about your mother."

"Excuse me, but... who are you?"

"My name is Walter. And I am pleased you have come to see me."

"Why?"

"So I can show you what your father has been doing. Maybe, after you have seen all that I want to show you, you will join us."

She looked around her at the stark white space. She couldn't tell from which direction Walter was speaking. She decided it was time to stop talking in generalities and asked a direct question.

"Are you and my father trying to take over the world?"

Walter laughed. "Let me show you."

The Adventure Continues...

Episode 7: Forgotten Reboot

Available February 3, 2014

Only Two Episodes Left!

Tell your friends to catch up on all the available episodes so you can discuss what you think will happen next!

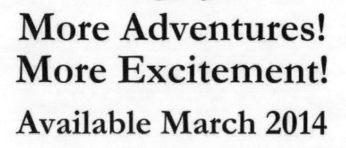

More Adventures!
More Excitement!

Available March 2014

S.D. Stuart's Minecraft Adventures Series

SEASON ONE RELEASE SCHEDULE

Herobrine Rises (Ep. 0 - 12/2/2013)

The Portal (Ep. 1 - 12/9/2013)

Day of the Creepers (Ep. 2 - 12/16/2013)

Here Be Dragons (Ep. 3 - 1/6/2014)

The Dark Temple (Ep. 4 - 1/13/2014)

Immortal Zombie (Ep. 5 - 1/20/2014)

Displaced Kingdom (Ep. 6 - 1/27/2014)

Forgotten Reboot (Ep. 7 - 2/3/2014)

Wither's Destruction (Ep. 8 - 2/10/2014)

Other books by S.D. Stuart

The Wizard of OZ: A Steampunk Adventure

The Scarecrow of OZ: A Steampunk Adventure

Fugue: The Cure

Minecraft Adventures: Series

Jason and the Chrononauts: Series (COMING SOON)

Writing as Steve DeWinter

Inherit the Throne

The Warrior's Code

The Red Cell Report (COMING SOON)

Be the first to know about Steve DeWinter's next book, and get your exclusive discount for each hot new release. In fact, receive your first exclusive discounts in the "Welcome" Email.

Follow the URL below to subscribe for free today!

http://bit.ly/BookReleaseBulletin